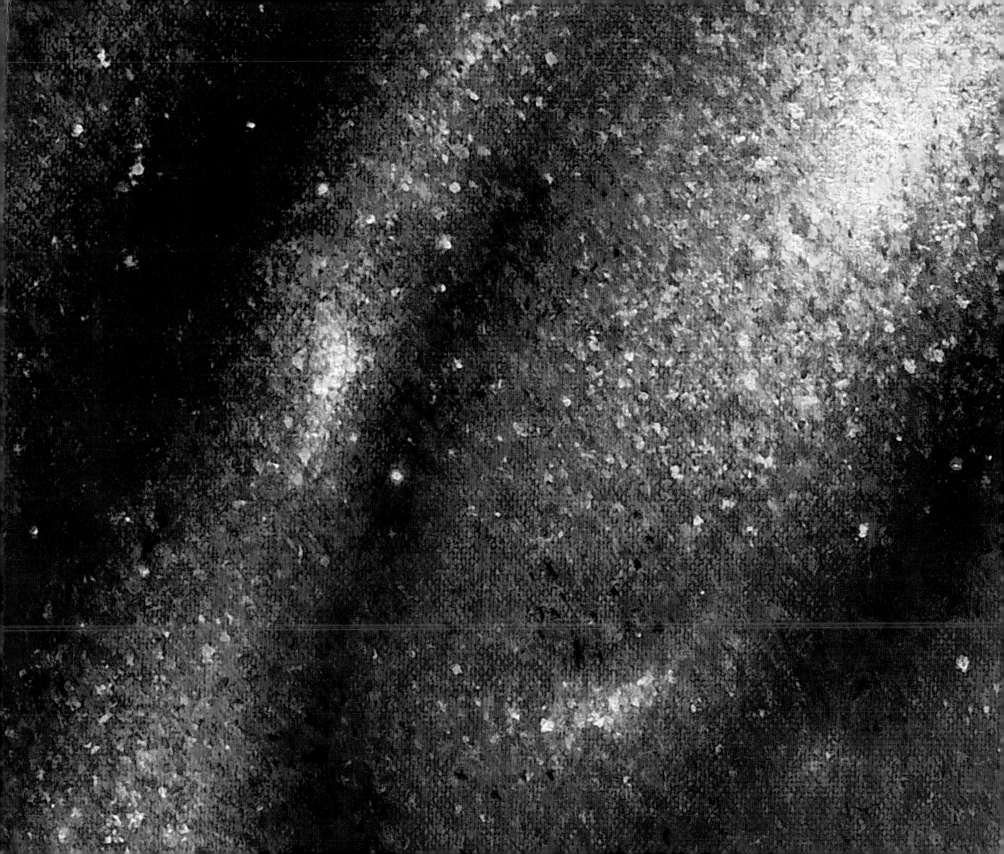

For Samuel,
with love ~ A. McA.

For L, Jackie, Betty
& Gwynfor ~ G. B.

PUFFIN BOOKS

Published by the Penguin Group

Penguin Books Ltd, 80 Strand, London WC2R 0RL, England

Penguin Putnam Inc., 375 Hudson Street, New York, New York 10014, USA

Penguin Books Australia Ltd, 250 Camberwell Road, Camberwell, Victoria 3124, Australia

Penguin Books Canada Ltd, 10 Alcorn Avenue, Toronto, Ontario, Canada M4V 3B2

Penguin Books India (P) Ltd, 11 Community Centre, Panchsheel Park, New Delhi – 110 017, India

Penguin Books (NZ) Ltd, Cnr Rosedale and Airborne Roads, Albany, Auckland, New Zealand

Penguin Books (South Africa) (Pty) Ltd, 24 Sturdee Avenue, Rosebank 2196, South Africa

Penguin Books Ltd, Registered Offices: 80 Strand, London WC2R 0RL, England

www.penguin.com

Published in hardback 2004
Published in paperback 2004
1 3 5 7 9 10 8 6 4 2

Text copyright © Angela McAllister, 2004
Illustrations copyright © Gary Blythe, 2004
All rights reserved

The moral right of the author and illustrator has been asserted

Set in Poliphilus MT

Manufactured in China

British Library Cataloguing in Publication Data
A CIP catalogue record for this book is available from the British Library
ISBN 0-670-91066-X Hardback
ISBN 0-140-56852-2 Paperback

Milo and the Night Market

Written by ANGELA McALLISTER

Illustrated by GARY BLYTHE

PUFFIN BOOKS

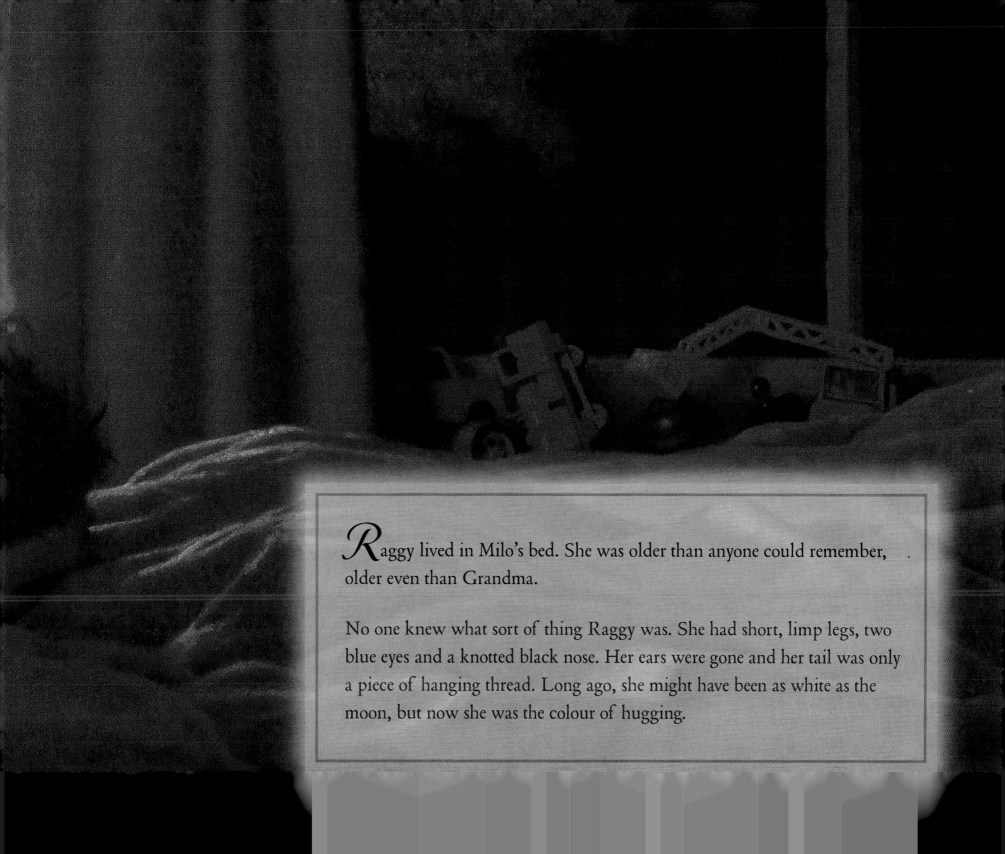

*R*aggy lived in Milo's bed. She was older than anyone could remember, older even than Grandma.

No one knew what sort of thing Raggy was. She had short, limp legs, two blue eyes and a knotted black nose. Her ears were gone and her tail was only a piece of hanging thread. Long ago, she might have been as white as the moon, but now she was the colour of hugging.

At night, inside his dark
burrow bed, Milo whispered stories
to Raggy and she told him secrets.
Was she simple or was she wise?
Only Milo knew.

One stormy night, Milo could
not sleep. The rowdy wind chased
the rain outside his window. Milo
crawled beneath the blankets,
curled around Raggy and told
her a story.

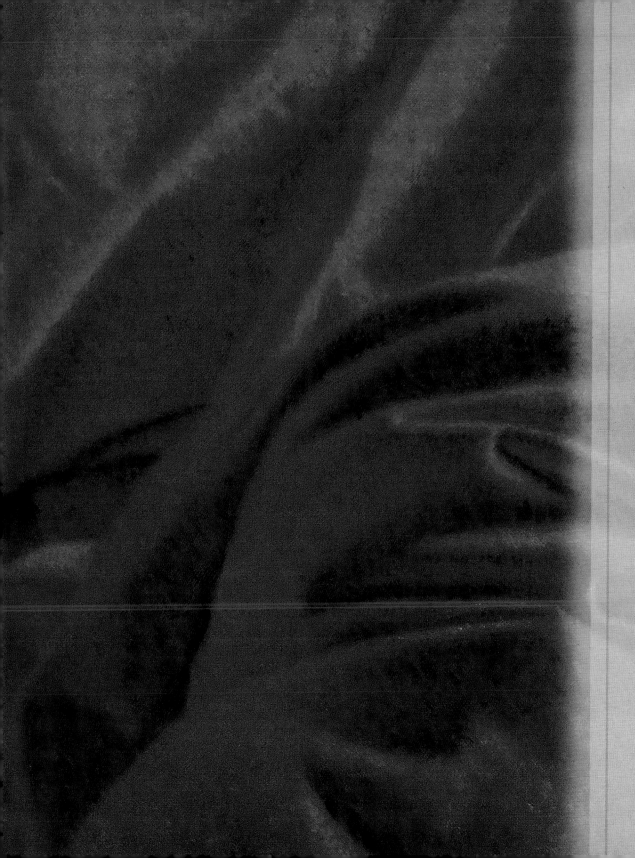

"Now tell me a secret, Raggy," said Milo with a yawn, "a long secret about sleeping . . ." The rain rattled the windowpane. Milo reached out for his friend. But Raggy was not there!

Milo hunted among the bedclothes. She wasn't this side or that. She wasn't upside or down. She wasn't anywhere at all. The harum scarum storm bucked and bellowed.

"Raggy!" cried Milo. "Where are you?" Where could she have gone on her old limp legs?

Milo turned and burrowed towards the end of the bed. Deeper and deeper he went, till the sound of the storm faded away. He felt about for Raggy but she was not there. He crawled on further still . . .

*S*uddenly Milo noticed stars twinking above his head. In the distance, lantern lights glowed. Milo stood up and walked towards them. Voices hummed and sang.

"We come to sell, we come to buy,
When stars are lit and moon hung high,
When moths and bats and barn owls fly,
When nightmares gallop and dreamers sigh,
We come to sell, we come to buy.
Nightmarket, nightmarket!"

*M*ilo stepped closer. The
nightmarket bustled with busy
creatures.

"Treats for a midnight feast!"
called a badger.

"Bedsocks blue, bedsocks green,"
chanted a vixen.

Milo joined the crowd. Curious people
jostled along with baskets and bundles,
but he could not see the tip of a
knotted black nose anywhere.

"Barrels of snores, barrels of snores!"
sang a hedgehog.

Milo tried a snore. He chose a
smooth round one and sucked it slowly.
"SSSNNNRRRGGHH!" and
"SSSNNNNNNNRRRGGHH!"
The snoring tickled his nose and
made him laugh.

Milo asked if anyone had seen an
old lost thing, but they all shook
their heads.

At one stall, Milo bought a golden dream for a pyjama button. At another, he tried glasses for seeing in the dark. When he put them on, he saw the shy, sly creatures of the night and the secrets of shadows. But he couldn't see two lost blue eyes.

$\mathcal{M}$ilo tried a silver net for catching falling stars.
He stopped to listen to a nightbird's song.
Then he spied the end of a hanging thread disappearing
behind a stall. "It must be Raggy, it must!" he gasped.
But when he chased around the corner, Milo found it was
only the tail of a moth-wing kite.

He jumped eleven moonbeams.
But he couldn't find Raggy.
Where was his friend?

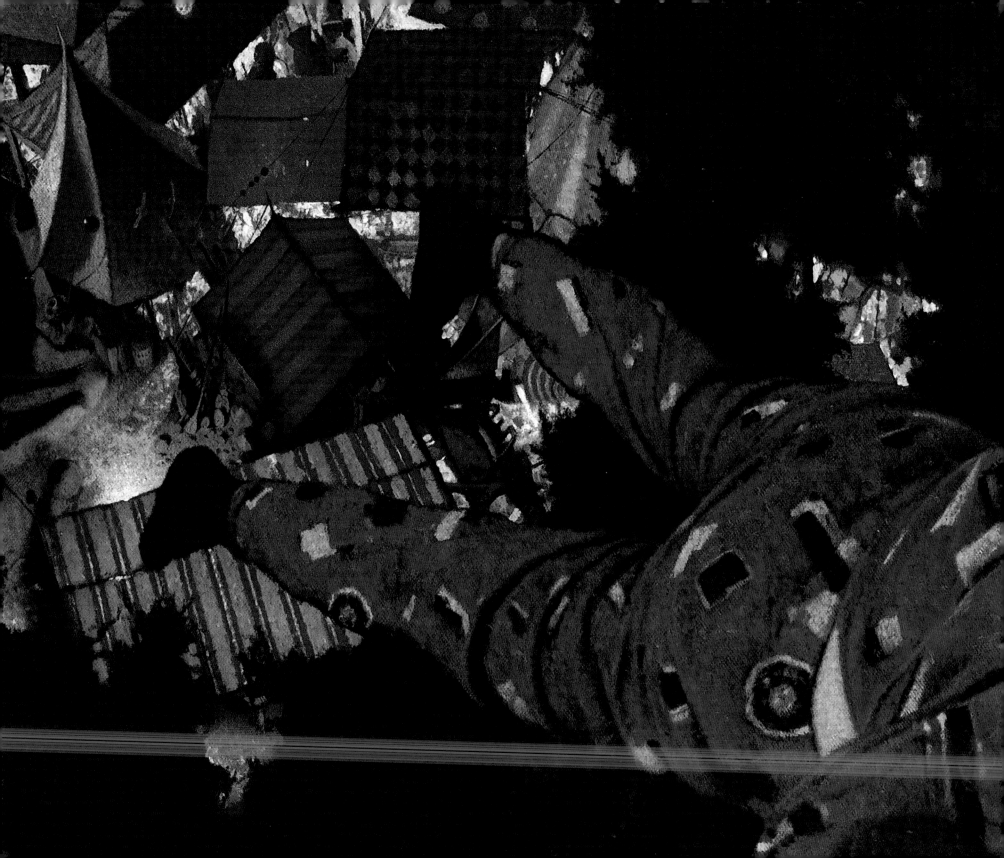

Under a tree lay copper pans heaped with coloured dust. An owl blinked. "Flying powder?" she said. Milo rubbed a handful into his heels and put on his glasses. Then he rose up, high into the night sky.

$\mathcal{M}$ilo saw comets and far spiral galaxies. He spun with satellites. He danced on the moon and peered into every crater, but he could not find Raggy. Slowly, sadly, he circled down, down to the nightmarket.

*G*low worms blinked. Milo yawned. Sheep in the lantern light bleated. Milo watched them jump over their fence. Over they jumped, round they skipped and over they jumped again. Milo began to count. As he watched and counted, he noticed one of the sheep looked familiar. Its eyes were blue, its nose was black and its tail was a raggy thread hanging . . .

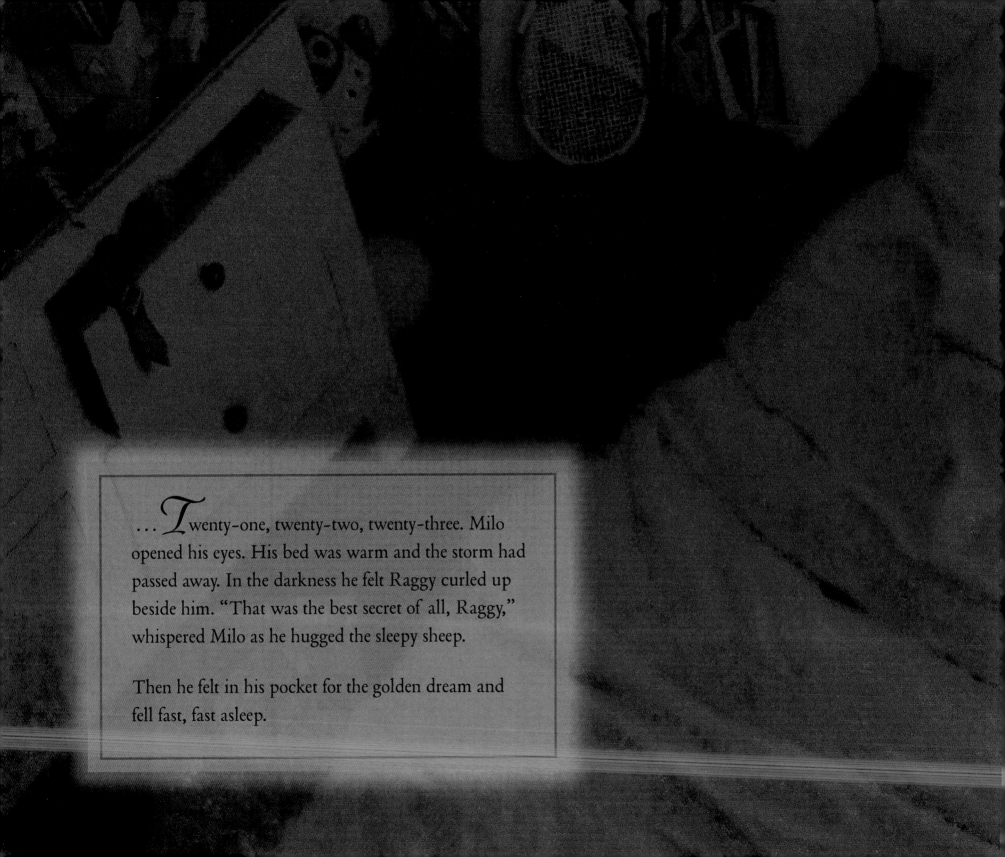

… $\mathscr{T}$wenty-one, twenty-two, twenty-three. Milo opened his eyes. His bed was warm and the storm had passed away. In the darkness he felt Raggy curled up beside him. "That was the best secret of all, Raggy," whispered Milo as he hugged the sleepy sheep.

Then he felt in his pocket for the golden dream and fell fast, fast asleep.

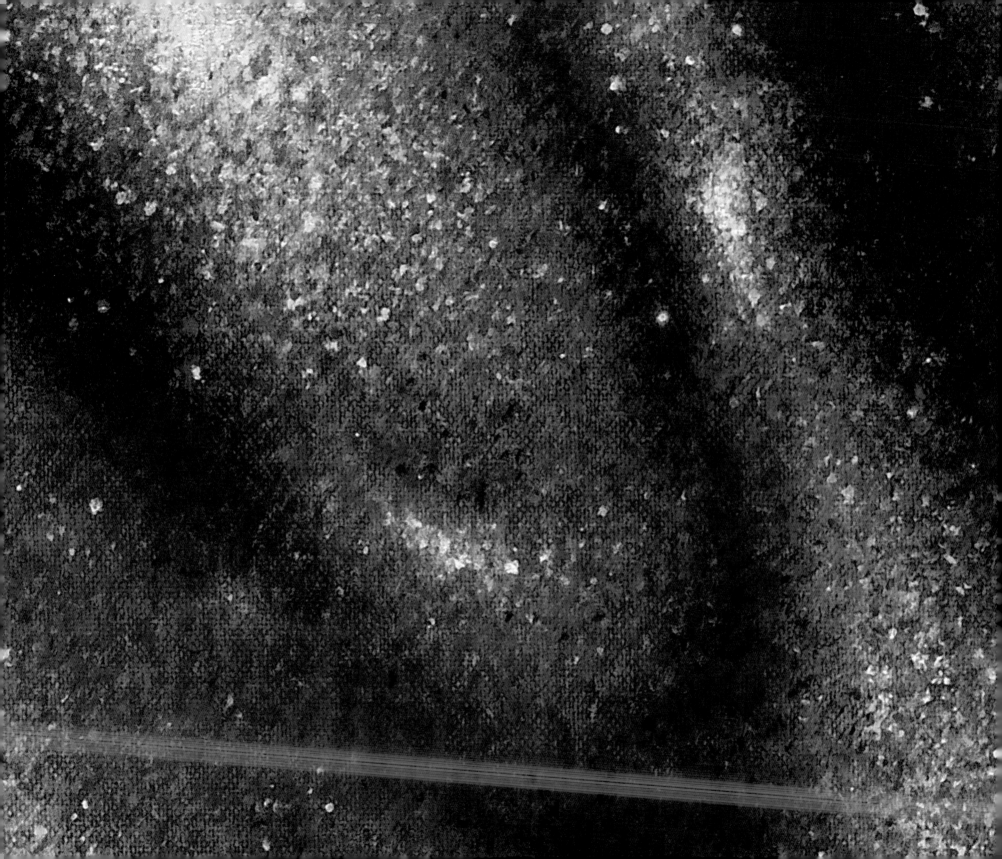

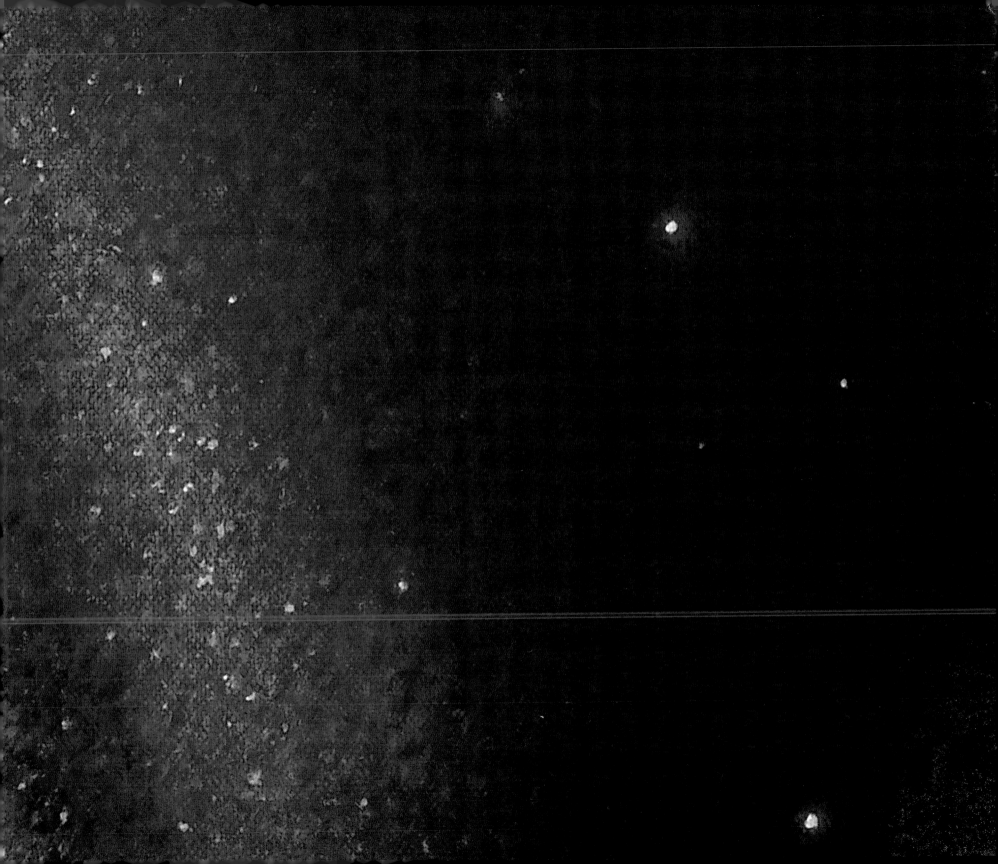